The House on the Hill

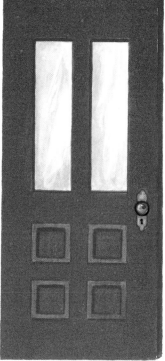

CHRISTIN COUTURE

FARRAR STRAUS GIROUX · NEW YORK

The author wishes to thank those who graciously opened
their homes and shops for browsing and sketching.

Library of Congress catalog card number: 90-27211
Published simultaneously in Canada by HarperCollins*CanadaLtd*
Color separations by Imago Publishing Ltd.
Printed and bound in the United States of America
Designed by Martha Rago
First edition, 1991

For Ray and Terry

The house stood on a hill.

Its bright red door could be seen from miles away.

Nobody ever came or went, so we decided nobody lived there.

One day, we had to go inside.

But we promised ourselves to go in only once.

What if somebody returned?

At first, we were a little frightened.

There were so many rooms to wander in.

Some of the rooms were large and empty;

others, small and enclosed.

There were so many things to do and see.

It was hard for us to choose.

Some were familiar.

But there was much that we had never seen before.

We played dress-up

and hide-and-seek.

We even made a snack.

Then we took a short nap.

In the basement, it was dark and cool.

Upstairs, in the attic, it was airy and light.

A trapdoor led to a room above.

It was the tiniest room of all, and we could see for miles.

It made us a little dizzy.

As twilight came, we saw the first star.

Some of us wanted to stay forever –

but we had our own rooms and treasures to return to.

So we put away the clothes and hats,

placed the books back on the shelves,

washed the dishes, packed the trunks,

smoothed the sheets, swept the floor,

put away the toys and games,

cleaned the bathtub.

We left the house just the way it was
and closed the bright red door behind us.